Brianna, Jamaica, and the Dance of Spring

Juanita Havill

Illustrated by Anne Sibley O'Brien

Houghton Mifflin Company
Boston 2002

For Mary Wong and her nieces Melissa and Kristin
—J. H.

For my dancers, Elizabeth, Maxine, Charlotte, and Olwyn
—A. S. O'B.

Text copyright © 2002 by Juanita Havill
Illustrations copyright © 2002 by Anne Sibley O'Brien

www.houghtonmifflinbooks.com

The text of this book is set in 16-point Sabon.
The illustrations are watercolor and pastel.

Library of Congress Cataloging-in-Publication Data

Havill, Juanita.
Brianna, Jamaica, and the Dance of Spring / written by Juanita Havill ;
illustrated by Anne Sibley O'Brien.
p.   cm.
Summary: When her sister Nikki gets sick, Brianna hopes to play her part as
the butterfly queen in the Dance of Spring, but then another disaster strikes.
ISBN 0-618-07700-6
[1. Dance—Fiction. 2. Sisters—Fiction. 3. Sick—Fiction.]
I. O'Brien, Anne Sibley, ill. II. Title.
PZ7.H31115 Br 2002   [E—dc21   00-056746

Manufactured in the United States of America
WOZ 10 9 8 7 6 5 4 3 2 1

Brianna stood straight and tall. She moved her arms in graceful arcs and leaped as high as she could. She hoped her dance teacher was watching.

At the end of class Jamaica ran up to Brianna. "I hope I get to be butterfly queen," she said.

"I think there should be two butterfly queens," Brianna said.

"The dancers in this class," Madame Moravec announced, "will be flowers and bees for the Dance of Spring." She gave each dancer a sheet of paper with a costume description.

"No fair." Brianna showed Jamaica her paper.
"I'm a sunflower."

Jamaica looked at her paper. "Marigold."
She frowned.

At home Brianna tried on her costume. "Hold still, Brianna. I don't want to poke you with a pin," her mother said.

Brianna stared in the mirror. Orange satin, black satin, and dark green tights. When it was her sister's turn to try on her butterfly queen costume, Brianna watched. "Mother, can I have wings on my costume like Nikki's?" she asked.

"You're a sunflower. You have petals," Nikki said.

"Bright orange petals," Mother said.

"Petals aren't the same as wings," Brianna said.

Every week at dance class Brianna and Jamaica practiced twirling like flowers in the breeze. Then Brianna stayed after to watch Nikki's class. Nikki leaped across the stage as if she were flying. Brianna tried to memorize every move.

At home Brianna practiced being a butterfly. She leaped down the hall and around her room.

One day when Jamaica came over, Brianna showed her Nikki's butterfly costume.

"Oh, wow!" Jamaica said. "Can I try it on?"

"Nikki's not home," Brianna said, "but I don't think she'll mind. I'll go first." Brianna put on the silky yellow gown with the black and yellow wings and the crown with velvet antennas. She danced the butterfly queen as if she were flying.

"You're as good as Nikki," Jamaica said.

"Here, you try." Brianna gave the costume to Jamaica. "But be careful."

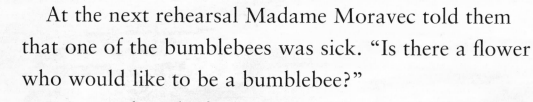

At the next rehearsal Madame Moravec told them that one of the bumblebees was sick. "Is there a flower who would like to be a bumblebee?"

Brianna thought for a minute. The bees had wings, little see-through wings.

Before Brianna could make up her mind, Jamaica held up her hand. "Beats being a marigold," she whispered to Brianna.

"Beats being a sunflower, too," Brianna said, but Madame Moravec didn't need any more bees.

On the Thursday before the recital, Brianna's mother picked her up after school. "Mother, where's Nikki? It's dress rehearsal today and all the classes dance together."

"Nikki's sick, Brianna. The nurse called me at lunch, and I came and got her. Dr. Shields is pretty sure it's strep throat."

"Oh no! What's Nikki going to do? She has to dance on Saturday."

"She's going to rest and get well. She'll dance another time. Could you give her costume to Madame Moravec?"

Brianna took the costume. She thought about the Dance of Spring. What would Madame Moravec do now?

"You will have to pay close attention," Madame Moravec told the dancers. "The butterfly queen is sick, and I have to change the dance to make it work without her."

"You don't have to," Brianna said in a soft, shaky voice.

"Brianna, did you say something?"

"I could be the butterfly queen. I've been practicing, and Nikki's costume fits me."

"Brianna's really good," Jamaica said.

Madame Moravec thought for a minute. Then she said, "As soon as you all have your costumes on, we'll begin. Brianna, let's see you dance the butterfly queen."

Brianna stood tall. The music started, and she began to zigzag around the flowers. Her gown swished and her wings trembled. Leaping and turning, she forgot about everything but the dance. When she finished, she felt that she had danced as gracefully as Nikki.

Madame Moravec asked her to stay after class to practice the steps again. Brianna danced from start to finish, and Madame Moravec didn't stop her once. No more Brianna sunflower. She was going to be the butterfly queen.

Brianna called Jamaica when she got home.

"I knew you could do it," Jamaica said.

"Beats being a sunflower," Brianna said. Then she went to tell Nikki about rehearsal. "You're not mad at me, are you, Nikki?"

"No," Nikki said, but she was frowning. "How did you know the steps?"

Before Brianna could even answer, Nikki said, "It's not fair. Why did I have to get sick? It's just not fair!"

"I hope you feel better tomorrow," Brianna said.

"It doesn't matter." Nikki flopped back on her pillow.

The next morning Brianna didn't feel good. She had a headache, her tummy felt queasy, and she wasn't hungry at all.

Her father felt her forehead. "Open your mouth wide, Brianna," he said, peering in at her throat. "It doesn't look too good."

Mother took her temperature. "We'd better have a throat culture done, Brianna."

"I feel fine," Brianna said.

When they got back from the clinic, her mother phoned Madame Moravec.

Brianna's head was spinning and her throat hurt when she swallowed.

After supper Jamaica called and told Brianna that Madame Moravec had changed the dance.

"Now there's no butterfly queen and no sunflower. I wish you didn't have to miss it."

But all Brianna could say was "Why did I have to get sick? It's not fair, not fair, not fair." After they hung up, she thought, *I sound just like Nikki.*

The night of the recital Brianna felt a little better. So did Nikki. They put on their robes and played games in their room.

As they crawled into bed, Brianna said, "I guess the recital is over now."

"I don't want to talk about dancing," Nikki said.

So Brianna didn't say what she was thinking. She waited for Nikki to fall asleep. Then she got up and took her sunflower costume from the closet and put it on. Humming quietly, she practiced the steps to her dance. Then she got back in bed.

Nikki woke her in the morning. "Brianna, did you sleep in your costume?"

Brianna nodded. "So I would remember my idea. We have costumes, Nikki. We can do our own recital." Brianna couldn't wait to tell Jamaica.

The next week they danced for their families. Nikki was a graceful butterfly queen in her yellow silk gown, and Jamaica danced the bumblebee again. Brianna sunflower twirled in the gentle breeze. Two orange petals trembled like wings on her back as she danced.